P9-CFH-732

15

Just the Facts

Teen Suicide

Claire Wallerstein

Heinemann Library
Chicago, Illinois

Customer Service 888-454-2279
Visit our website at www.heinemannlibrary.com

Designed by Jane Hawkins
Originated by Ambassador Litho Ltd.
Printed and bound in China by South China Printing Company

07 06 05 04 03
10 9 8 7 6 5 4 3 2 1

Library of Congress Cataloging-in-Publication Data
Wallerstein, Claire, 1969-
    Teen suicide / Claire Wallerstein.
       p. cm. -- (Just the facts)
    Contents: What is suicide? -- Suicide across history and cul-
ture -- Who commits suicide? -- Suicide hot spots -- The explo-
sion in youth suicide -- Which teenagers are at risk? -- Possible
causes -- Does suicide run in families -- Parasuicide -- Copycat
suicides -- The role of the media -- Euthanasia and assisted suicide -- When suicide goes wrong -- Surviving a suicide attempt
-- What happens to those left behind -- Myths about suicide --
Tackling teenage suicide -- What to do -- Legal matters -- Treatment and counseling.
    ISBN 1-4034-0820-3 (Library Binding : hardcover)
    1. Teenagers--Suicidal behavior--Juvenile literature. 2. Suicide
--Juvenile literature.   [1. Suicide.]   I. Title. II. Series.
HV6546.W35 2003
362.28'0835--dc21

2002010942

Acknowledgments
The author and publisher would like to thank the following for permission to reproduce copyright material:
Cover photograph: Getty Images (main image); MPM Images (background).
p. 4 Bettman, Reuters/Popperfoto; p. 5 Stockmarket/Corbis; p. 7 Ancient Art and Architecture; p. 9 Peter Newark; p. 10 Michael Lewis/Corbis; pp. 11, 14, 28 Topham Picturepoint; p. 13 Brendan Beirne/Rex Features; p. 15 Phanie Agency/Rex Features; p. 17 Gary D. Landsman, Stockmarket/Corbis; p. 18 Gregg Newto, Reuters/Popperfoto; p. 19 John Birdsall; p. 21 Nina Berman/Rex Features; p. 22 David Allocca/Rex Features; p. 23 Tim Rooke/Rex Features; pp. 25, 36 The Image Works/Topham Picturepoint; p. 26 Rex Features; p. 29 PressNet/Topham Picturepoint; p. 30 Reuters/Popperfoto; p. 32 Kathy McLaughlin, The Image Works/Topham Picturepoint; p. 33 Detroit Free Press/Associated Press; p. 34 Annabella Bluesky/Science Photo Library; p. 35 Digital Vision; p. 37 Hodder Wayland Picture Library; p. 39 Phil Rees/Rex Features; p. 40 APM Studios/Hodder Wayland Picture Library; p. 42 Novosti/Topham Picturepoint; p. 43 Topham Picturepoint; p. 45 Popperfoto; p. 47 Ray Tang/Rex Features; p. 48 Giacoma Pirozzi/Panos; p. 49 Angela Hampton/Hodder Wayland Picture Library; p. 50 Mug Shots, Stockmarket/Corbis.

Every effort has been made to contact copyright holders of any material reproduced in this book. Any omissions will be rectified in subsequent printings if notice is given to the publisher.

Our special thanks to Pamela G. Richards, M.Ed., for her help in the preparation of the book.

Some words are shown in bold, **like this.** You can find out what they mean by looking in the glossary.

Contents

What Is Suicide?

Growing up can be difficult. Although some people sail through their teenage years with few worries, others find it harder to cope. Problems such as exams, bullying, or constant arguments with someone close may make them feel angry, stressed, or frightened. In a few cases, people may feel so bad they even end up committing suicide. Deep down inside, they usually do not really want to die. But death may look like the only way of stopping what seems like endless misery.

Famous suicides

All types of people, including the rich and famous, may be struck by suicidal feelings. The ancient Egyptian queen Cleopatra, for example, allowed herself to be bitten by a poisonous snake more than 2,000 years ago. More recently, rock star Kurt Cobain took his own life in the 1990s.

Kurt Cobain, lead singer of the grunge band Nirvana, battled with depression and a drug habit for many years before finally taking his own life in 1994.

Suicide is strongly linked to depression. Sadly, many suicidal people do not even realize that they are suffering from this common medical condition that can usually be successfully treated.

The suicide rate

Today, at least one percent of all deaths around the world is from suicide. In 2002, according to the World Health Organization, nearly one million people died from suicide. That means that every 40 seconds one person committed suicide. In the United States, suicide kills twice as many people annually as AIDS. The suicide rate among adults has been rising quite slowly in most countries. But the picture is very different among young people, especially among young men. The suicide rate among people aged 15 to 24 in most **industrialized countries** has tripled or even quadrupled since 1960.

As a result, youth suicide is a concern for governments and doctors today. Yet they are still far from understanding all of the reasons behind this massive increase. This is partly because many adults still find it hard to accept or understand that young people could want to kill themselves.

ff The world was so dark, it seemed the sun never came out. When I picture that time in my mind, it is always darkness. JJ

(Anonymous U.S. teenager who attempted suicide, discussing her feelings on a website)

Suicide in History

The way in which we think about suicide has changed greatly throughout history. In the past, many people mistakenly saw it as a heroic act. In ancient Greece and Rome, for example, people did not think the way they died was important, as long as it was with honor. Criminals were often offered the choice of suicide as an alternative to execution. Similarly, the Scandinavian Vikings believed that warriors who died in battle would receive the greatest honors for bravery in the afterlife. They were closely followed by those who committed suicide.

The sin of suicide

In the early days of Christianity, suicide was common among some strict religious groups. In the 4th and 5th centuries, the religious group known as the Donatists, for example, wanted to get to heaven as soon as possible without waiting for a natural death. They were famous for throwing themselves off cliffs in huge numbers, or paying complete strangers to kill them.

By the 6th century, church leaders were so worried by the number of deaths that they declared suicide a sin. A person who committed suicide was buried at a crossroads. A stake was driven through his or her heart. It was believed the person could not enter heaven without a Christian burial. People who tried to kill themselves, but failed, were executed. This practice continued in some countries such as England, until the 19th century. In 1993, Ireland became the last European country to get rid of the old laws declaring suicide a crime.

According to Orthodox Jewish teachings, suicide is as bad as murder, except in some extreme cases. In 73 c.e., for example, 960 Jews on the clifftop of Masada, Judea, faced capture by the Romans after a long siege. Rather than allowing themselves to be captured, they committed mass suicide by jumping to their deaths.

Other religious views

Other major religions look harshly on suicide, too. According to Islam, people who commit suicide are condemned to hell, as only Allah (God) can say when we should die. One big exception is *jihad*, a "holy war" to protect Islam. In this case, people who commit suicide believe they will become martyrs and that Allah will reward them with great gifts in heaven. A group of terrorists who claimed to be fighting such a *jihad* killed themselves, along with more than 3,000 innocent people, during the attacks in New York and Washington, D.C., in September 2001. Most Muslims, however, disagree strongly with such acts of violence.

People of many Eastern religions, such as Buddhism and Shintoism, believe in reincarnation—the rebirth of the soul in another body. Because of this belief, suicide is not viewed as harshly.

A certain type of ritual suicide, called *suttee,* was actually expected of Hindu women in India and was only banned in 1829. If a woman's husband died, the woman was supposed to throw herself on his funeral pyre (the bonfire burning his body) to show her grief.

In this ancient carving, a Roman falls on his sword. For people who lived in a violent age when many people died young, suicide was seen as a dignified death.

Religious cults

Sometimes, people have committed mass suicide after being brainwashed by religious **cults.** In 2000, hundreds of members of a cult in Uganda locked themselves in a church and set it on fire. They had been told the end of the world was coming.

Protest suicides

Some people use suicide as a drastic means of protest, when they feel there are no other options. For example, Thich Quang Duc, a Buddhist monk, set fire to himself in the Vietnamese city of Saigon in 1963. He wanted to protest against the government's poor treatment of Buddhists.

Hara-kiri

In other cases, suicide has been seen as a matter of dignity. In Japan, for example, a type of suicide called **hara-kiri** developed in the 16th century. It involved a very elaborate ceremony. The person committing hara-kiri, which means "belly slit," had to **disembowel** himself—pull out his intestines—with a sword. Then an assistant would chop off his head.

The last well-known person to commit hara-kiri was the writer Yukio Mishima in 1970.

Today, suicide may still be expected in a few **hunter-gatherer societies.** People who live in rain forests and other wild places survive by hunting animals and gathering fruits and vegetables. Because they do not farm crops, it can sometimes be difficult to find enough food. Old and sick people, who can no longer help provide for the group, may be expected to kill themselves if supplies run low.

❝Death is before me today. Like the recovery of a sick man ... like the longing of a man to see his home again after many years of captivity.❞

(The earliest known discussion of suicide, in a fragment of ancient Egyptian writing dating back to 2100 B.C.E.)

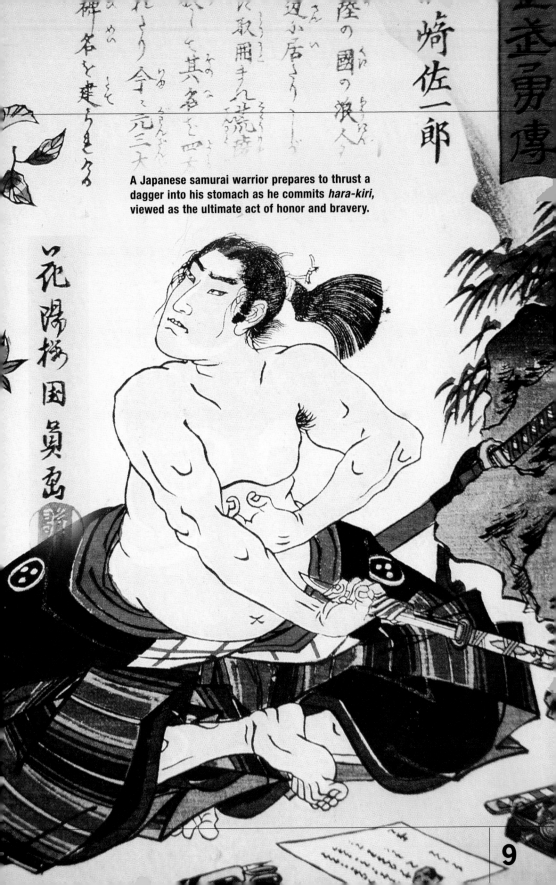

A Japanese samurai warrior prepares to thrust a dagger into his stomach as he commits *hara-kiri*, viewed as the ultimate act of honor and bravery.

Who Commits Suicide?

People in some countries are more likely to commit suicide than in others. For example, rates are very high in the former Soviet republics. There, people have had to cope with high unemployment and other problems since the collapse of the Communist system in 1991. Developing countries seem to have much lower suicide rates. This may be because many people lead more traditional lifestyles than in the West and may have stronger family relationships. It probably also has much to do with the authorities' failure to keep good records about what people have died from.

Countries colonized relatively recently, such as the United States, Canada, Australia, and New Zealand, have high rates of suicide. This may be because people do not have the same shared history and sense of belonging that exists in "older" countries.

Factors in suicide

Ethnicity can also have an effect. In the United States, for example, the suicide rate is highest among white people. However, the number of African Americans and Mexican Americans committing suicide is rising quickly, especially among young people. Suicide rates among African-American children between the ages of ten and fourteen rose almost 300 percent between 1980 and 2002.

People of certain professions, such as veterinarians, dentists, doctors, and farmers, are particularly likely to commit suicide. In addition to their stressful jobs, it is easy for them to obtain guns, pesticides, or dangerous drugs. Veterinarians and farmers often destroy sick or useless animals. They may see this as the best option for themselves, if they feel they are also useless.

Age is important, too. The highest suicide rate is among elderly people, especially white men over the age of 75. They often suffer from serious illnesses or are moved into nursing homes that may make them feel lonely and depressed. However, most suicides, in terms of actual numbers, happen among young people. In the United States it is the third leading cause of death among 15- to 24-year-olds.

Gender also plays a role. Women and girls are more likely to suffer from **depression** than men and are roughly three times more likely to try to commit suicide. Yet, about six times as many males as females actually succeed in killing themselves. This is because men tend to use more violent methods. Women are more likely to overdose on drugs and can often be treated in a hospital.

Religion could be a factor. In places where suicide is forbidden, such as in Muslim countries, it seems not to exist. But this could be because embarrassed families say the death was from another cause. In Europe, there are usually lower rates in Catholic countries than in Protestant ones, which take a milder view of suicide.

Family links

There are certain patterns to suicide. Writing in the late 1800s, French **sociologist** Émile Durkheim blamed the Industrial Revolution for the rapid rise in suicide. As people moved from villages in the countryside to cities, religion, tradition, and family links were broken down. He said this could lead to **depression** and suicidal urges.

This still seems to hold true today. People without strong social or family contacts—such as single, divorced, and widowed people—have a higher than average risk of committing suicide. There are more suicides at certain times, such as at the beginning of the week and during holidays, especially Christmas and Valentine's Day. At these times, depressed people may feel lonelier than at other times. Most teens kill themselves at home in the afternoon or early evening.

Many **Aborigines** have lost their traditional way of life and survive in miserable conditions at the edges of society in Australia—one of the world's richest countries.

❝The pace of life is faster than ever now. There is academic pressure, peer group pressure to get involved in things like drugs, pressure to find a good job and, for young men especially, our society still expects them to have a stiff upper lip.❞

(Samaritans, an international support organization, chief executive Simon Armson)

Loss of culture

In Australia, the rate of suicide among young Aborigines, once almost unheard of, is four times higher than among the general population. A 1994 study suggested that these high rates stem from Aboriginal people being forced out of their ancestral lands by European settlers and losing their traditional culture. They have often been unable to adjust to modern life. Aborigines suffer high rates of unemployment and poverty. This in turn can lead to higher rates of alcoholism, drug abuse, family violence, and sexual abuse. All of these are risk factors for suicide. The situation is even worse among **indigenous** youths in North America, while in New Zealand the government has set up a special suicide prevention program for young **Maoris.**

Suicide Hotspots

Japan

In Japan, suicide has traditionally been seen as an honorable way of dying. For example, **kamikaze** pilots in World War II felt proud to crash their airplanes into enemy targets. In recent years, a major economic slump in Japan has led many people, especially middle-aged men, to take their own lives after losing their jobs or being unable to pay off debts.

A do-it-yourself guide, *The Perfect Suicide Manual*, was on the bestseller lists in Japan for years before it was finally banned. There are several suicide websites, too. A small forest on the slopes of Mount Fuji near Tokyo has attracted many suicidal people. In 1998, 70 bodies were found in the forest. The local authorities then put up signs saying: "Think of the pain you will cause your family before you take any drastic action."

Thousands of young Japanese pilots, like the one in this plane about to crash into the USS *Missouri* in 1945, killed themselves trying to destroy enemy ships. *Kamikaze* means "divine wind."

❝The trains are often delayed because of suicides. When people jump, it takes hours to get to the office.❞

(Female commuter traveling on the so-called "suicide line" railway in western Tokyo, where many people have taken their own lives)

Finland

One of the reasons behind the high rate of suicide in Finland could be a type of **depression** called **seasonal affective disorder (SAD).** It is caused by the lack of ultra-violet light found in sunshine. During the long, dark months of the Scandinavian winter, the Sun only rises above the horizon for a couple of hours each day. SAD symptoms include feelings of despair, depression, disrupted sleep, and lack of energy. SAD is most common in women and can affect people in any country with low levels of winter sunlight. There are an estimated ten million sufferers in the northern United States.

SAD can usually be helped with **phototherapy,** a treatment with bright ultra-violet lamps. This is offered by the medical services in Scandinavian countries. Many cafés also have the lamps. Finland has a very high rate of alcohol abuse, another risk factor in suicide.

Phototherapy lamps work by mimicking the Sun's rays and tricking a person's body into believing that winter has already passed.

In the United States, an average of twelve young people kill themselves each day. One in three teens now knows someone who has attempted suicide. The picture in Canada is similar. It is even worse in Australia and New Zealand, where only traffic accidents cause more youth deaths.

And the figures may be even higher. In some countries, such as the United Kingdom, coroners (the officials who carry out inquiries after deaths) can record a verdict of suicide only if suicide is proven "beyond all reasonable doubt." This means that some car accidents involving only one vehicle are recorded as "accidental deaths," but may actually be suicide. Similarly, some "accidental" drug overdoses may be suicides.

Depression

In some surveys, roughly half of young people in Western countries say they suffer from loneliness and **depression** from time to time. Doctors do not fully understand why depression seems to be rising so quickly, but point out that only a very few depressed people will actually kill themselves.

Although girls are still the most likely to attempt suicide, the rate of suicide is actually going up much faster among boys than girls. This is mainly because boys use more violent methods. It may also be because many traditionally male jobs in farming, fishing, or manufacturing have disappeared. This may make some boys feel hopeless about their future.

It may also be harder for boys to seek help than for girls. Boys may bottle up their feelings and might turn to alcohol or drugs for comfort. In a 2001 survey by the international organization Samaritans, twenty percent of young people said they would laugh if a male friend told them he was depressed.

Schoo
best o
life, o
goes.
more
these
enorm
and a
a viol
soluti
proble

Considering suicide

In a 2000 survey of more than 25,000 U.S. students, 12 percent said they had seriously considered suicide in the previous year. Of those who had considered suicide, 37 percent actually tried to kill themselves during that period. Females (16 percent) were almost twice as likely as males (8 percent) to be at risk for suicide, according to the study.

"I won't talk about a lot of things close to my heart with friends ... most boys wouldn't. Boys tend to want to be in a strong position ... deal with it yourself—lump it or leave it."

(Nineteen-year-old man in a hostel in London, 2001)

Teens at Risk

Nearly everyone who is suicidal is depressed. **Depression** may be caused by something obvious, such as suffering from abuse or the death of a parent. Often it has no clear reason at all. It can make people feel utterly miserable, as if an endless black cloud is hanging over them. Very few depressed people actually kill themselves. However, other problems in their lives can sometimes act like a trigger, pushing them to thoughts of suicide.

Homelessness

Homeless children have a high risk of committing suicide. Many of these teens have run away from problems at home such as sexual or physical abuse or big arguments with parents or stepparents. They may become victims of violence or abuse from other people living on the streets. This can deepen their anxiety and depression.

Alcohol and drugs

Many teens use alcohol or drugs to help them forget about their problems. However, alcohol and drugs can make depression worse and affect a person's ability to think clearly. One young person in every three who commits suicide is drunk or on drugs.

"We used to hear of suicides on the news, but now they're so common they aren't reported."

(Anonymous fifteen-year-old interviewed about youth suicide by the Scout Association of Australia)

Homeless people, such as these people sleeping on the ground in Brazil, have a stressful and uncertain life. They are at the mercy of the weather and may be harassed by police or beaten up by criminals.

Some bullies physically attack people. Others tease and pick on their victims all the time, making them feel lonely, frightened, and depressed. Often it is so bad that death seems like the only way out.

Problems at school

Other children who may become suicidal are perfectionists or over-achievers at school. Their parents, or they themselves, may set extremely high standards. They may not be able to cope with the pressure. Some may be victims of bullying. There is at least one bullying-related suicide, or **bullycide,** each month in the United Kingdom alone. Although official bullycide statistics are not kept in the United States, up to two-thirds of U.S. students experience bullying at some point.

Risk factors for suicide include:

- Breaking up with a girlfriend/boyfriend or having had an **abortion.**
- Being in prison. It can be difficult and frightening to cope with being locked up for a long period of time, sometimes with older, hardened criminals.
- Homosexuality. Teens coming to terms with being gay are ten times more likely to commit suicide than others their age. They may feel under pressure to "live a lie" and keep their sexuality a secret from friends and family.

Underlying Causes

Nearly all people who kill themselves have some kind of mental illness, usually **depression.** But having such an illness does not make a person "crazy." In fact, at least one in four people will suffer from depression at some stage in their lives. It is often because the chemicals in the brain have gotten slightly out of balance. Sometimes depression creeps up so slowly that people do not realize anything is wrong. They think it is normal to always feel miserable.

Mental illness

Although most people who commit suicide are depressed, it is important to remember that very few depressed people actually commit suicide. In fact, many of today's most successful celebrities and role models suffer from depression. As well as depression (also called **unipolar affective disorder)**, other less common problems linked to suicide also often start to appear in the teenage years. These are **manic depression (bipolar affective disorder)**, **schizophrenia,** eating disorders, alcoholism, and drug abuse. Illnesses such as depression can make people less able to cope with difficulties, such as important exams and relationship problems.

Finding it hard to cope with problems has nothing to do with intelligence. It has more to do with how a person views the world. Some people may see a stressful event as an exciting challenge, but it might make a depressed person feel totally desperate. People suffering from a mental illness are between five and fifteen times more likely to commit suicide than the population as a whole. With schizophrenia, a voice may actually command the person to kill him or herself even though that person does not want to die.

Successful treatment

The good news is that these illnesses can usually be successfully treated. Unfortunately, some young people are too frightened or embarrassed to ask for help. Although 90 percent of young people who kill themselves have some kind of mental illness, only 15 percent are actually getting treatment at the time of their death.

"Sometimes I think about killing myself. It's not that I want to die. I don't. But sometimes just being alive hurts so much that I would do anything to make it stop."

(Lisa Marie, a teen talking about her depression on the Psyke website)

Anorexics have a kind of mental illness that makes them obsessed with dieting and controlling their body weight, even when they are dangerously thin. Many anorexics suffer from depression.

Guide to Mental Illnesses

We now know that having a mental illness is no more someone's fault than catching a cold. It does not help to tell a depressed person to "snap out of it." Mental illnesses are usually caused by a problem with a person's brain chemistry, which can be treated. Below are some of the most common mental illnesses.

Depression

Although many people suffer from **depression** at some stage, for some people it has no obvious cause and cannot be shaken off. Even young children can suffer from depression.

Eating disorders

People with eating disorders become completely obsessed with their weight. **Anorexics** starve themselves, sometimes to the point of death. Those suffering from **bulimia** will binge on food and then get

Singer Fiona Apple takes regular medication for depression, and says her illness has been the inspiration behind her music.

Princess Diana was one of the world's richest and most glamorous women. Yet she was plagued by bulimia and depression.

rid of it by taking **laxatives** or making themselves vomit.

Manic depression

People with **manic depression** experience huge mood swings, ranging from a desperate low to an elated high, or mania. In manic periods, the person may be **hyperactive,** be very busy, and not need much sleep. Roughly one percent of the population suffers from this condition at some point.

Depression diagnosis

To be diagnosed with depression, a person will have at least five of the following symptoms for at least two weeks, in addition to feeling continuously down:

- inability to sleep or sleeping too much
- appetite change, weight loss or gain
- mental and physical slowness
- inability to concentrate or make decisions
- loss of energy
- feeling worthless or guilty
- frequent thoughts of death or suicide.

Schizophrenia

The rare condition **schizophrenia** has a wide range of symptoms known as **psychosis.** People become unable to tell the difference between what is real and unreal. Paranoid schizophrenics may suffer **hallucinations** and **delusions.** They may become convinced that someone is spying on them or trying to kill them. Disorganized schizophrenics may talk nonsense. They may be **catatonic—** rigid and hardly moving—or hyperactive. Schizophrenics may find it hard to make friends or keep a job.

High-Risk Families?

While scientists do not believe there is a suicide **gene,** people in some families do seem to have a higher than average risk of committing suicide. It seems faulty genes may be passed on from generation to generation. These cause chemical imbalances in the brain and can lead to **depression** and, occasionally, to suicide. The risk of depression can be up to 70 percent if a person's identical twin (who is genetically identical) also suffers from it. This occurs even if the twins were given up for adoption and grew up in different families. **Manic depression, schizophrenia,** and eating disorders also have a genetic link. The genetic link means that scientists may one day be able to cure some mental illnesses. By using **gene therapy,** they hope to be able to remove or correct the damaged genes.

However, many other factors are involved. Eating disorders, for example, were rare 100 years ago, and so cannot be blamed on genetics alone. In fact, the glorification of very thin supermodels seems to have played a bigger role.

A gloomy outlook?

Children of depressed parents may learn by example to have a gloomy outlook on life. It is also possible that some family suicide clusters happen simply because the traumatic death of a child or close relative can make life seem unbearable, even for people who have never

A genetic factor may mean some of these partygoers could get hooked on alcohol more easily than others. If they are depressed, alcohol could make things worse.

previously felt depressed. So it is important to remember that no one is "doomed" to commit suicide. The genetic link simply means some people may have a greater tendency to do so. Suicide is very complex, and people do not commit suicide just because of one particular feeling or problem.

Serotonin

Scientists at the Royal Ottawa Hospital in Canada have found that **DNA** from most suicidal patients has a mutation that healthy people do not have. This affects the production of **serotonin,** a chemical in the brain that controls mood. In other experiments, rats killed their own babies when serotonin levels in their brains were lowered.

Parasuicide

Parasuicide is when people make a suicide attempt, but do not actually want to kill themselves. It is sometimes called **deliberate self-harm.** Usually, these people take an overdose of pills and then call a friend or an ambulance. Or they may carry out the act in a place where they hope to be found and helped. However, this does not always happen. Help may not arrive until it is too late.

Parasuicide is not the same as when people deliberately harm themselves in less serious ways. For example, some people may cut themselves when they feel very stressed or upset. This is not life-threatening, and they do it because they believe the pain somehow helps them.

A call for help

Parasuicide is often a cry for help from people, usually girls, who have trouble coping with their problems. They suffer from the same kind of difficulties as those who actually do commit suicide.

People who commit parasuicide, like this French woman who drove her car into a crowd of soccer fans, may do so to show how much they are hurting inside.

They may feel it is the only way to make the people around them understand how bad or how angry they are feeling. Some teenagers commit parasuicide because they want to frighten someone who has upset them and "make them sorry." This is very dangerous because some parasuicides end in death.

Parasuicide also shows how confused many suicidal young people are. They may want to take drastic action or even kill themselves, but often change their minds quite quickly. Few people are 100 percent certain that they want to die. Even when they feel at their worst, there is nearly always a part of them that clings to life.

People who commit parasuicide may be told they are attention-seekers or time-wasters. Their families may be very angry and upset, making the person feel even more miserable and guilty. However, people who have committed parasuicide should be taken seriously. They are likely to try it again, and are up to twenty times more likely than the general population to finally take their own lives.

Copycat Suicides

It is thought that one young person in every twenty who commits suicide could be copying the death or suicide of someone else, often an idol such as a pop star or movie star. In one famous case in 1933, Kiyoko Matsumoto, a nineteen-year-old student, dramatically threw himself into a 1,100-foot (335-meter) deep volcanic crater on the island of Oshima, Japan. In the following months, 300 other teenagers did the same thing at the same place.

Most young people spend time fantasizing. They may be told they are always daydreaming or "have their head in the clouds." Some identify so strongly with a person—often a pop star they have never met—that life may seem impossible without that person if he or she dies. Hollywood movies often glorify the idea of "living fast, dying young," rather than growing old and "fading away."

For some young people, the early deaths of famous people, such as Marilyn Monroe, film star James Dean, 1960s rock star Jimi Hendrix (pictured left), and Nirvana singer Kurt Cobain, can seem romantically tragic. Many copycat suicides are among people of the same sex or age as the person being imitated. Copycats particularly seem to identify with the person if the death is portrayed as "senseless" or the "inexplicable act of a healthy person" that has left everyone baffled.

> **"Most people, in committing a suicidal act, are just as confused as when they do anything important under emotional stress. Carefully planned acts of suicide are as rare as carefully planned acts of homicide [murder]."**
>
> (Erwin Stengel, suicide investigator, United Kingdom)

Ozzy Osbourne

Heavy metal singer Ozzy Osbourne was sued in the 1980s by the parents of one of several fans who killed themselves while listening to his song "Suicide Solution." However, Osbourne was finally cleared by the courts. He said the song had been written about a friend who died while drunk. The word *solution* was supposed to mean "liquid," not "answer." No matter how upset the families were, he said, the fans had become suicidal because of problems in their lives—not because of his music.

Ozzy Osbourne may be famous for biting the heads off live bats, but he has said that people do not commit suicide because of his music.

The Role of the Media

Many researchers believe that high-profile news reports of deaths may push vulnerable or depressed people to commit copycat suicides. In one year in the 1970s, for example, there were 60 suicides by burning in the United Kingdom after reports of a woman burning herself to death in Switzerland. Such suicides are normally extremely rare.

These deaths create a problem for journalists. Dramatic suicides are worth reporting. They usually interest readers a lot more than run-of-the-mill stories about government politics. Suicide prevention organizations are trying to teach journalists to write about suicides more sensitively.

The way in which the media portray suicide can have a huge effect on some depressed or vulnerable people.

For example, when newspapers stopped their sensational reporting of suicides on the subway in Vienna, Austria, the number of such suicides fell from thirteen in 1986 to just three in 1989.

Spare us the details

The United Nations (UN) published reporting guidelines in 1996, advising the media not to focus on the hopelessness of the dead person's life or make suicide seem glamorous. They were told not to endlessly repeat the story or describe the method used. However, there is still a long way to

go. In July 2001, the *New York Post* was criticized for a front-page story with the headline: "Model found dead in pool of blood." It went into great detail about how the woman had killed herself.

TV dramas

The stories in television dramas can have an important influence on young people. They send out dangerous signals if a child's suicide is shown to have a positive result, such as shaming school bullies. However, hospital dramas can be useful. For example, they can teach young people about the dangers of overdosing on **painkillers.**

Kurt Cobain

Suicide experts expected a big wave of copycat suicides after the lead singer of the band Nirvana, Kurt Cobain, killed himself in 1994. However, there were actually very few. This may have been due to the sensitive and low-key media reports and the publication of hotline telephone numbers in the press. Thousands of young people did call these hotlines to talk to counselors in the weeks following Cobain's death. It seems they got over their grief by talking about it, rather than actually ending their own lives.

Euthanasia

The word *euthanasia* means "good death" in Greek. Most euthanasia is carried out for people who are **terminally ill** with diseases such as cancer. They want to die before they start to suffer great pain, lose their mental abilities, or become totally dependent on others. In assisted suicide, a friend or doctor supplies the patient with the means to end his or her life, such as a large number of sleeping pills.

Mercy killing

In the case of euthanasia, or mercy killing, people have already become too ill to kill themselves. A doctor would have to act for them. A doctor might act passively by stopping treatment, such as turning off a life-support machine. Alternatively, a doctor may actively end the patient's life, such as by injecting a poisonous drug.

Today, euthanasia is legal in only one state, Oregon. There are concerns about it because people may say they want to die, but their sickness may have made them unable to think clearly. Euthanasia causes problems for doctors, whose job is not only to preserve life but also to stop suffering. Some doctors have broken the law and helped terminally ill patients to die.

Caring for and befriending terminally ill people can help them to make the most of their last days, months, or years.

> **"I believe often that death is good medical treatment, because it can achieve what all today's medical advances and technology cannot achieve—and that is to stop the suffering of the patient."**
>
> **(Christiaan Barnard, South African surgeon who performed the world's first heart transplant)**

Dr. Death

Probably the most famous person linked with euthanasia is Dr. Jack Kevorkian (pictured above right), often called "Dr. Death." He devised a machine called the *thanatron* (Greek for "death machine"). It has switches that allow patients to inject themselves with lethal drugs. Dr. Kevorkian said his machine made death "dignified, humane, and painless and the patient can do it in the comfort of their own home at any time they want." When the authorities stopped him from buying the necessary drugs, he helped his patients kill themselves with poisonous carbon monoxide from car exhaust fumes. After assisting an estimated 130 people to end their lives, Dr. Kevorkian was jailed for murder in April 1999.

Failed Suicide Attempts

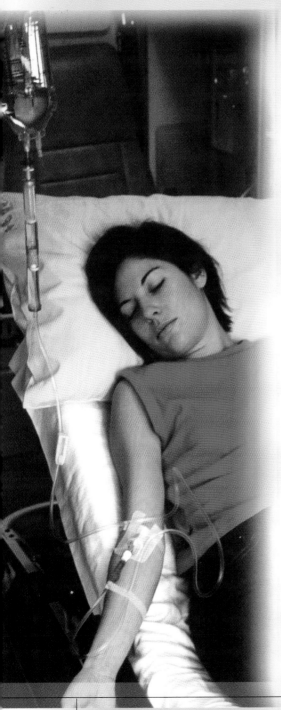

Experts believe that for every suicide there may be up to 100 failed attempts. However, people who have survived a suicide attempt will not necessarily walk away unharmed.

More than 50 percent of young women who attempt suicide do so by taking an overdose of **painkillers.** Within a short time, they may change their minds and be glad to find they are still alive. However, they often do not know that these drugs take many hours to be absorbed by their body.

If they get to a hospital quickly, doctors may make them eat a mix of gooey black charcoal to remove the poison. Unlike in the movies, stomach pumping, in which a hose is forced into the stomach and the contents sucked out, is rare. Stomach pumping is not only painful, but it can also cause death if stomach acid gets into the lungs.

Specialist treatment

If the overdose took place more than four hours before, patients are hooked up to an **intravenous drip** for 32 hours to help flush out the poison. They will later need treatment from a specialist. Painkillers are often toxic to the liver so they may even need a liver transplant.

Without enough transplant organs to go around, a person who attempts suicide may be less likely to get a transplant than a person with liver disease. This means a certain number of people will die within a month of taking an overdose.

Another less common problem of failed suicide attempts is permanent paralysis, or loss of the ability to move or feel. This can happen to people who have survived jumps from tall buildings or intentional automobile accidents. Some people have even survived after shooting themselves in the head. They usually have brain damage or partial paralysis similar to someone who has suffered a stroke. Their faces are usually disfigured or destroyed.

Time to change their minds

Suicide prevention groups in Australia are putting up fences around bridges and other structures that people often jump from. Similar projects have been completed at suicide hotspots such as the Golden Gate Bridge in San Francisco (below). Researchers say these barriers create delays that may make suicidal people change their mind or give rescuers time to reach them.

Surviving an Attempt

However miserable things can seem to a person who is suicidal or has just survived a suicide attempt, it is important to remember that life can get better. Many people have tried to commit suicide, but have gone on to achieve great things in life. For example, Mark Twain, author of *Tom Sawyer* and *Huckleberry Finn*, once put a loaded revolver to his head, but could not bring himself to pull the trigger. Some survivors go on to become counselors, helping other young people who are going through similar problems.

Help to heal

Post-traumatic stress disorder is common among suicide survivors, and they need counseling to help deal with this. They might suffer either from frightening memories or flashbacks of

> **"I'm glad I didn't succeed at suicide. There are good times now that I would not have had, and the people who love me—it would have taken away a piece of their lives, too. It's selfish to kill yourself."**
>
> (Jim Shanley, a young American who tried, and failed, to kill himself)

Suicide survivors may be teased by those who do not understand what drove them to it.

the attempt, or they might lose their memory of it altogether. They might feel anxious and guilty. Survivors may not want to talk about what happened, but this does not mean that they have gotten over it. Recovery takes time, so people should not be told to "pull themselves together" or that it is "all in the past."

Suicide stigma

People who have tried to commit suicide will probably be **depressed.** They are more likely than the population at large to try to kill themselves again, especially in the first three months after an attempt. The danger may not fully pass for some years. There is still a **stigma** about suicide. Survivors often find that their friends or family do not know how to cope with what has happened. They may react with anger or place all the blame on themselves. Others might avoid survivors because they do not know what to say. They may pretend it has not happened and refuse to talk about it.

The People Left Behind

Often, parents and families are forgotten after a young person's suicide or suicide attempt. Yet they, too, can suffer from **post-traumatic stress disorder.** This may be worse if they were the one to find the body, were with the person as they died, or watched **paramedics** trying to revive him or her. Family members will often have to identify the body in a hospital morgue, the storage room for dead bodies. They may even have to clean up the place where the person died.

In the weeks, months, and years after the suicide, loved ones try to come to terms with strong emotions such as shock, confusion, and anger. Their friends and neighbors may not know what to say or may even blame the family for what happened. Close friends or family members may fall into deep **depression** and attempt suicide themselves. Professional counseling can be helpful for them.

Understanding why

One of the most difficult things for those left behind is trying to understand why the teen committed suicide. Roughly fifteen percent of teens who commit suicide leave a note. Unless the person wrote down his or her feelings in a diary, there may never be any way of knowing the reasons for the suicide. Unlike in cases of natural death, such as from illness, the parents and family often find they cannot fully get over a suicide. They are left wondering if there was anything they could have done to prevent it.

Sometimes families who have lost a young person to suicide find it helps to design the headstone or plant a memorial tree. They might make a website dedicated to the person or keep a diary about their feelings.

"You spend your whole time trying to understand why he chose death instead of life, whether we were at all to blame, and why he did not tell his father or me— who would have given our own lives to save him had we only known."

(Anne Parry, a science teacher whose son killed himself in 1994)

Myths About Suicide

Although we are slowly learning more about suicide, it is still a subject often surrounded by lies, confusion, and secrecy. This can be dangerous, because it can mean a person's suicidal feelings may not be recognized or taken seriously until it is too late.

It is very important, therefore, to separate the facts about suicide from the myths.

Myth: People who threaten to commit suicide do not try to kill themselves.

Fact: Eight out of ten people who commit suicide have said they feel like dying.

Myth: People who kill themselves really want to die.

Fact: Most suicidal people are not sure whether they want to live or die. Suicide is often a cry for help during a crisis.

Myth: Once the **depression** seems to lift, the danger is past.

Fact: This can be the most dangerous stage. If something goes wrong now, it can make the person feel even worse. Their apparent calm may be due to relief after finally deciding on suicide.

Myth: If someone talks about suicide, it is important to get his or her mind off it and change the subject.

Fact: By talking openly with him or her, a friend will make the suicidal person feel that he or she is being taken seriously. If the friend finds out the person has a definite plan for suicide, it is important to get help quickly.

Myth: Someone who has tried to kill himself or herself will not do it again.

Fact: At least 30 percent of teen suicides have made a previous attempt.

Myth: Threatening suicide is a type of emotional blackmail that should be ignored or punished.

Fact: All suicide threats should be taken seriously.

Myth: Suicide sometimes comes "out of the blue."

Fact: No one ends their life for no reason, although the warning signs may be hard to recognize.

Myth: If someone swears a friend to secrecy about a suicide plan, that person must not tell anyone about it.

Fact: Someone who helps another person to kill himself or herself is not a good friend. Someone who knows about a person's suicidal plan should get help for that person.

Myth: If the suicidal person is in counseling or therapy, he or she is safe.

Fact: Roughly fifteen percent of teens who commit suicide are undergoing treatment at the time of their death.

[Male] Doctor: "You're not even old enough to know how bad life gets." Cecilia: "You've never been a thirteen-year-old girl."

(From the movie *The Virgin Suicides*, about five young sisters who committed suicide in the 1970s)

Tackling Teen Suicide

The United Nations (UN), World Health Organization (WHO), and governments in most Western countries recognize youth suicide as a major problem. The UN has suggested that governments should set up programs to deal with all the factors linked to suicide, such as mental illnesses, youth unemployment, child abuse, drugs, and alcoholism. However, in developing countries suicide is often still a taboo issue that is not discussed.

In many schools in the United States, teachers are trained to identify students who appear unhappy. Students are taught problem-solving and confidence-boosting skills. Most schools also have programs to crack down on bullying. There are also efforts to reduce suicide in prisons. Young inmates are helped by a **psychiatrist** and put on suicide watch if they are thought to be at risk. They are checked hourly during the night.

Suicide prevention

In the United States in May 2001, the Surgeon General outlined the country's first-ever national strategy for suicide prevention. A key issue involves training doctors and nurses to recognize the early signs of **depression** and mental illness among young people. Then they can offer treatment before the problems become severe.

Australia's $20 million youth suicide prevention strategy, set up in 1995, partly focuses on teaching families better parenting skills. New Zealand's strategy, In Our Hands, was launched in 1998. It hopes to limit access to the means of committing suicide, such as guns, and to offer more support to families with "at-risk" children.

In the United Kingdom, the government aims to reduce the suicide rate by one-fifth by 2010, and has set up special counseling lines for young men in areas of high male unemployment. In Ireland, a special task force was set up in 1995 to raise public awareness of the factors involved in suicide.

Young offenders need a wide range of activities to keep them fit, active, and mentally alert to avoid sinking into depression while in detention.

Removing the poisons

Many studies have shown that removing access to the means of suicide has led to a big decrease in the overall suicide rate. For example, the poisons were removed from oven gas in the 1960s. **Catalytic converters** make exhaust fumes less toxic in cars. In the United Kingdom, some **painkillers** are sold only in packs of sixteen. This is thought to reduce the risk, but it is important to remember that these are extremely dangerous drugs.

What to Do

Health professionals look for particular signs in someone they think might be suicidal. Spotting these is often difficult. However, some warning signs include saying things such as: "I won't be a problem for you much longer" or "It's no use." The person may say "I won't see you again" or complain of feeling "dead inside."

People might start to prepare for the suicide by giving away precious possessions or cleaning their bedroom. Their eating and sleeping habits may change or they may stay away from friends and family. They might give up activities they once enjoyed, such as sports, music, or going to the movies.

On the other hand, people who are planning suicide could seem unusually happy, panicky, or agitated. They might take a lot of risks, such as driving too fast. They might rebel against their parents or teachers. Other risk signs include suffering from **hallucinations,** or developing obsessions about particular things, such as washing hands or losing weight.

Caring for the suicidal

If a person seems likely to attempt suicide soon, experts advise the following:
- Do not leave the person alone. Suicidal people may ask their parents, brothers, or sisters to leave the house so they can carry out the suicide.
- Try to keep the person talking until the crisis has passed.
- Get help by calling for an ambulance, the police, or a trusted adult.

If a person has survived a suicide attempt, it is important to do these things:
- Keep a careful eye on him or her, but do not be overprotective.
- Do not force the person to talk about the suicide attempt. Only discuss it if it is brought up.
- Get back to the regular family routine as soon as possible.
- Remove any dangerous substances or weapons, such as guns, rope, poisons, and medicines. The risk of suicide is much lower if the means of suicide are removed. For example, in the United States, where many people keep guns at home, about 60 percent of suicide victims shoot themselves. There are hardly any such deaths in the United Kingdom, where guns are illegal.
- Get professional help and advice. It is important to face problems and not sweep them under the carpet.

Some people at risk of suicide might not appear to be **depressed** at all. In fact, they might seem very energetic and the "life of the party."

Legal Matters

Suicide is no longer illegal in many Western countries. The major legal issue, therefore, concerns **euthanasia**—stopping treatment for sick people or injecting them with a drug to make them die. This includes assisted suicide, in which sick people are given the means to kill themselves, such as a large amount of drugs. Euthanasia is illegal nearly everywhere and can result in a murder charge and a possible life sentence in prison. Assisted suicide also often carries a heavy penalty, although less severe than for euthanasia cases.

However, courts often treat people who have assisted a suicide less harshly than cold-blooded murderers. They may be sympathetic if it is clear the person was suffering unbearable pain and really wanted to end his or her life. In most places, passive euthanasia is legal. Patients can choose to refuse treatment that is keeping them alive.

Living wills

Some people make living wills that may be written or recorded on a videotape or audiotape. They state their wish for passive euthanasia if they are unable to give permission for it, for example, if they have fallen into a coma. If a patient has made a living will, the doctor who helps that patient to die is less likely to be prosecuted.

The only country where active euthanasia is legal is the Netherlands. In the United States, the state of Oregon passed a "Death with Dignity Act" in 1994 that allows assisted suicide if death is likely within six months. However, attempts to pass similar laws in Michigan (1998), California (2000) and Maine (2000) all failed.

Legal euthanasia

Since 2000, doctors in the Netherlands have been allowed to give overdoses of drugs to people with a "concrete expectancy of death." However, the regulations are strict to make sure the law is not abused. Doctors may also carry out euthanasia on **terminally ill** children above the age of twelve, although those under sixteen must get their parents' permission. Neighboring Belgium seems likely to legalize euthanasia in the near future, too.

Terminally ill Diane Pretty, who was no longer able to move or speak, begged the British and European courts to allow her husband Brian to give her a lethal dose of drugs. Her requests were turned down. She finally died in 2002.

Treatment and Counseling

Many organizations exist to help suicidal people find an alternative to ending their lives. People who get help before they make a suicide attempt are likely to recover better and quicker than those who never tell anyone about how they feel until after they have tried to kill themselves.

However, some suicidal teens may feel frightened or embarrassed about seeking professional help. They may be drug users or in trouble with the law or mistakenly think that counseling is only for people who are "crazy." There is no shame in seeking help. Being **depressed** is fairly common and does not mean a person is "crazy."

Talking

It may seem simple, but talking is one of the best ways of dealing with depression and suicidal feelings. People who can open up and talk about the troubling things going on in their lives often find it easier to work out a solution to their problems. People who feel hopeless and keep everything bottled up may become more and more convinced that there is no solution.

Many depressed people feel that those around them do not understand their problems or will not listen. However, there are dozens of professional groups who will listen in confidence.

They will not tell anybody, although they may contact the police if they think a person is going to hurt himself or herself or someone else. Many counselors have had similar problems themselves. They will not be angry if a person admits to feeling suicidal and will take his or her problems seriously.

Hotlines

Hotlines are usually available 24 hours a day to help people who are going through a crisis. Since the conversations are anonymous, hotlines are often used by people who are not yet ready to talk to a doctor or counselor.

Many organizations now have e-mail counseling services that are very popular with young people. Teens may feel more comfortable getting help via the Internet rather than face-to-face. The Samaritans' website even has a button that can be clicked to make the Samaritans' logo disappear. This means that in a public place, nobody else will realize the person is using a counseling service.

Schools

Many schools in the United States and Australia have suicide-prevention programs. Schools may also have special counselors trained to help young people with their problems. If not, a trusted teacher can usually offer a sympathetic ear or give advice about how to find professional help.

Religious leaders

Religious leaders, such as priests, ministers, and rabbis, can help, too. They may be able to give a more spiritual view of how to overcome problems. For some people, religious faith can help them see life's problems as part of a bigger picture, making some kind of sense of their difficulties.

Psychotherapy

Some people find professional **psychotherapy** is the most helpful way to sort out their suicidal feelings. The therapist talks to a person about what is making him or her **depressed** and how to cope with the difficulties of daily life. The person learns how to fight off depression if it returns.

Drug treatment

A doctor may treat a suicidal person with antidepressant drugs, as well as refer him or her for professional therapy. The drugs can give a person some breathing room to decide how to tackle his or her problems. Modern antidepressants, such as Prozac, are not thought to be habit-forming. But they are powerful drugs that affect the brain's chemistry. There may be some side effects, usually when a person starts to take them. These may include nausea, dizziness, insomnia (inability to sleep), and the feeling of living in a dream. More serious and rare conditions, such as **manic depression** and **schizophrenia,** can also be treated with drugs. The earlier people get treatment, the less likely they are to commit suicide.

Treatment centers

Doctors or therapists may also refer people to treatment centers. There they will receive help in kicking their alcohol or drug habit, which might have played a large role in their depression or suicidal feelings. However, this treatment will not work unless the person really wants to give up the habit. He or she will receive counseling and gradually lowered doses of replacement drugs.

Emergency services

In extreme cases, the police can restrain people to stop them from killing themselves. Emergency service workers, such as ambulance workers and **paramedics,** will resuscitate (revive) people. They will take them to a hospital where doctors will do everything possible to keep them alive. After treatment, **psychiatrists** will keep an eye on them until it is safe for them to go home. Very agitated people may be kept sedated, or put on drugs to keep them calm.

Information and Advice

The following organizations and websites can offer information and support for people who are depressed and suicidal, and for their friends and families. Many of them give advice on how to get through some crisis areas in teenage life, such as school exams.

Suicide contacts

American Association of Suicidology
4201 Connecticut Avenue NW, Suite 408
Washington, D.C. 20008
(202) 237-2280
http://www.suicidology.org
This association is dedicated to the understanding and prevention of suicide.

American Foundation for Suicide Prevention
120 Wall Street, 22nd Floor
New York, NY 10005
(212) 363-6237; (888) 333-AFSP
http://www.afsp.org

Befrienders International
http://www.befrienders.org
This organization has 1,700 crisis centers and hotlines worldwide. There are more than 31,000 volunteers working in 41 countries, providing 24-hour telephone and confidential e-mail counseling.

Suicide Awareness Voices of Education (SAVE)
Minneapolis, MN 55424
(952) 946-7998
http://www.save.org
SAVE is dedicated to educating people about suicide prevention.

Suicide Prevention Action Network of USA (SPAN USA)
5034 Odins Way
Marietta, GA 30068
(888) 649-1366
http://www.spanusa.org
SPAN USA's goal is to save lives through suicide prevention. On their website is a bounty of information for teens and adults.

Yellow Ribbon Suicide Prevention Program
P.O. Box 644
Westminster, CO 80036
(303) 429-3530
http://www.yellowribbon.org

Hotlines

National Adolescent Suicide Hotline
(800) 621-4000

National Child Abuse Hotline
(800) 4-A-CHILD (800-422-4453)

National Drug and Alcohol Treatment Hotline
(800) 662-HELP (800-662-4357)

National Youth Crisis Hotline
(800) HIT-HOME (800-448-4663)

Suicide Hotline
(888) 333-2377

More Books to Read

Friedman, Michelle S. *Everything You Need to Know about Schizophrenia.* New York: Rosen Publishing Group, Inc., 2000.

Kelly, Pat. *Coping with Schizophrenia.* New York: Rosen Publishing Group, Inc., 1999.

Kuehn, Eileen. *After Suicide: Living with the Questions.* Mankato, Minn.: Capstone Press, Inc., 2000.

Peacock, Judith and Jackie Casey. *Depression.* Mankato, Minn.: Capstone Press, Inc., 2000.

Peacock, Judith. *Teen Suicide.* Mankato, Minn.: Capstone Press, Inc., 2000.

Schleifer, Jay. *Everything You Need to Know about Teen Suicide.* New York: Rosen Publishing Group, Inc., 1999.

Wallerstein, Claire. *Depression.* Chicago: Heinemann Library, 2003.

Glossary

Aborigine original people of Australia, who were living there before European settlers arrived

abortion procedure carried out to end a pregnancy

anorexic person suffering from *anorexia nervosa*, a mental illness. Sufferers become obsessed with their body weight and starve themselves, sometimes to the point of death.

bipolar affective disorder also known as manic depression. Sufferers have periods of severe depression and periods of heightened energy, excitement, and happiness (mania).

bulimia eating disorder in which sufferers often gorge themselves on huge amounts of food and then make themselves vomit or take laxatives to get rid of the food

bullycide suicide committed as a result of being bullied

catalytic converter attachment in a car that uses chemicals to make a car's exhaust fumes less toxic

catatonic condition suffered by some patients with schizophrenia, in which they become rigid and cannot move

cult group, usually religious, that follows a strange or extreme belief system, often led by one powerful leader

deliberate self-harm when someone hurts themselves on purpose. They may cut themselves because it gives them a sense of relief at a stressful time.

delusion fixed, but false, belief. Schizophrenia sufferers often have delusions and believe, for example, that someone is spying on them.

depression medical condition in which a person feels very miserable over a long period of time. A person with depression is said to be *depressed*.

disembowel to remove the innards or guts from a person or animal

DNA (deoxyribonucleic acid) genetic material inside the cells of all living things

euthanasia type of assisted suicide in which a terminally ill person is helped to die

genetic relating to genes. *Genes* pass on characteristics from parents to children such as eye color, height, or the likelihood of developing certain diseases.

gene therapy new type of medicine in the early stages of development. In the future, scientists hope that faulty genes, such as those that cause certain diseases, could be "turned off."

hallucination seeing things or hearing noises that are not real

hara-kiri type of suicide dating back to 16th-century Japan. A person cuts open his stomach with a special sword to remove the intestines, and then a friend chops off his head.

hunter-gatherer society group of people who live mostly by hunting and fishing and collecting wild food

hyperactive extremely energetic, much more than normal

indigenous original, or native, people in countries such as the United States, Canada, Australia, and New Zealand, who were living there before European settlers arrived

industrialized country rich, developed country, such as the United States, Australia, Japan, and European countries, with an economy based on high-tech manufacturing rather than farming

intravenous drip usually a sugar-salt solution that passes directly into a vein through a needle

kamikaze name of Japanese pilots in World War II who crashed their planes into enemy targets, killing themselves in the process

laxative drug that relaxes the muscles of the bowels, allowing the body to get rid of waste food before it has been fully absorbed

manic depression *see* bipolar affective disorder

Maori native people of New Zealand

painkiller something, such as a drug, that relieves pain

paramedic type of medical professional. Paramedics often arrive in ambulances and are usually the first on the scene in an emergency.

parasuicide act that appears to be an attempted suicide, but was probably not intended to be successful

phototherapy treatment with bright, ultra-violet light lamps to treat seasonal affective disorder (SAD)

post-traumatic stress disorder condition often suffered by people following a very stressful or traumatic event, such as a suicide attempt

psychiatrist type of doctor who specializes in mental illnesses

psychosis symptoms typical of schizophrenia patients, such as delusions, hallucinations, and mental confusion

psychotherapy professional therapy through which people are helped to understand what led to their depression

schizophrenia mental illness caused by a chemical imbalance in the brain, in which a person suffers from psychosis and has an increased risk of suicide

seasonal affective disorder (SAD) type of depression caused by a lack of the ultra-violet light found in sunlight

serotonin chemical in the brain that, among other functions, controls mood

sociologist person that studies how human society works

stigma shame or disgrace linked to a certain person or subject, usually through ignorance

terminally ill suffering from an illness that cannot be cured and will eventually lead to death

unipolar affective disorder *see* depression

Index